Mom's Number Rules

Donnetta McCormick

AuthorHouse™
1663 Liberty Drive
Bloomington, IN 47403
www.authorhouse.com
Phone: 1 (833) 262-8899

This book is printed on acid-free paper.

ISBN: 978-1-7283-7028-6 (sc)
ISBN: 978-1-7283-7029-3 (e)

Print information available on the last page.

Published by AuthorHouse 08/27/2020

author**HOUSE**

Mom's Number Rules

Hey little Dinjer, tomorrow you start school.

Let's have another talk about mouse traps and rules

We'll talk about everything you need to know

So you'll be prepared when it's time to go.

Now these are mouse traps
with powerful teeth

Before you can get its cheese the
strap must be released. You
may see these traps
over here or over
there Wherever
you see them son
always beware

Now, I've packed you some tools that you're going to need remember you can be anything you want to be.

The next morning Dinjer leavwes home through a crack in his wall

He enters a house with such a long hall.

He runs down the hallway
as fast as he can

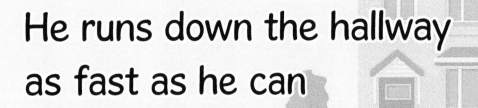

Passing the first trap
under a table stand

I'll go to the next
trap, oh, I'll get
that cheese!

He enters a
bathroom with a
big cat that's
sleep

Under the tub Dinjer could see two
mouse traps. Yet, he was afraid
to wake the cat from its nap.

He left the bathroom went
further down the hall
where he saw an opened
door that stood so tall

Inside of the door, were
coats and hats

on the very top shelf were
three mouse traps

The shelf looked
so high, real
high in the air

Dinjer wondered
and thought, I can't
get up there!

He left the coat closet and
entered a living room

Four traps in each corner,
surrounded by brooms

Dinjer became happy saying
I'll now make my stand

Before he could get
started, in walks
a woman

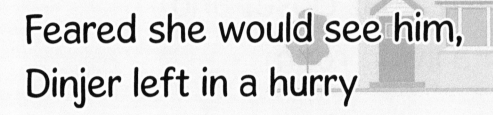

Feared she would see him,
Dinjer left in a hurry

For the woman was huge and
her face looked so scary

He entered another
room with a washer
and dryer

As he approaches
the machines their
voices got higher

Under the washer were five traps in a row. From fear of its noise he decided not to go

A smell entered his nose, a smell his mom never mentioned

He followed that smell which led him to a kitchen

He saw six traps, some over
here and over there

Remember when you see
this son always beware.

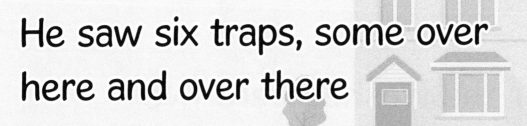

Dinjer looked around,
everything
looked alright

Until he was
spotted by a cat
with a large
appetite

Dinjer ran till he tumbled
down the basement stairs

Then hid between two boxes
behind some old chairs.

He peeked between the
boxes and saw seven
traps with cheese

Dust filling his nose,
trying his best not
to sneeze. Ha... Ha....
Ha...... Hachooooo!

Up jumped the cat saying......
"Oh, I see you !

Dinjer took off running
       fast, fast, fast,

       Jumped through
         a crack in the
         wall where he's
         safe at last.

He climbed up the wall until he reached the attic

No cheese to take home, poor Dinjer starts to panic.

As he sat on the attics floor beginning to cry

Accomplishing nothing, not understanding why? Through the fog of his tears, he could hear his mom say. Son, obey my rules, use these tools then you'll be okay

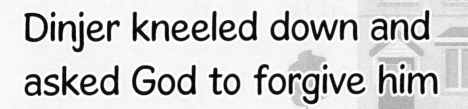

Dinjer kneeled down and
asked God to forgive him

for not obeying the rules he
was taught by mom to live in.

God then provided
Dinjer with strength,
courage and wisdom

To finish the
journey that he
had been given.

wiping his eyes, pulling out his tools. Saying,

"I'm going to get that cheese, I'm obeying mom's rules".

The big woman put all the cats outside as she went out to explore

A clear path had been given to Dinjer, that wasn't there before.

Dinjer collected all the cheese with the help of angels he couldn't see, heading home with the largest smile on his face

learning God's rules are
here to keep us all safe

Dinjer burst in the house
yelling Mom I am home

I did it! I did it mom
all on my own

Mom gave the warmest
smile Saying welcome
home little Dinjer

Sit down, let us talk all about your adventure.

Just like Dinjer's mom, God gives us rules to obey

We'll run into trouble doing things our own way

When Dinjer realized he didn't obey mom's rules for living

He prayed and asked God if he could please be forgiven

God forgave Dinjer while clearing a path for him to succeed using the tools mom had given, Dinjer collected all the cheese obeying God could provide us with a protection of grace

God's rules are here to help us and to keep us all safe.

By: Donnetta McCormick

Dedicated To, Markel McCormick